This book is given with love:

To:

✗ _____

From:

✗ _____

Skritchy Beard

A Misfit Pirate's Tale of Teamwork

Created by April & Jackson Jones

When Skritchy Beard was a kitten, he heard many stories,

Of pirate captains far and wide, and their many glories.

Daring crews on sturdy ships, sailing out to sea,

And all the trials that they faced, living lives so free.

Our young Skritchy Beard set out on his first quest,
Went down to the harbor, to find a ship and all the rest.

All too quick he found his plans had a few small flaws.
He did not have a single coin, in his furry paws.
He traveled up and down the docks, all day and night too,
Asking for a ship to have, any ship would do!

But all the people that he asked, all sounded just the same,
"Oh little cat, the seas are harsh, it's not some kind of game.
All the ships that you see here we need to make a living.
We haven't any ships to spare, especially ones for giving."

And so the day seemed to drag, ever slowly by,
Until the story finds our hero sitting down to cry.
"What is wrong my furry friend?" asked a tiny voice so small,
Skritchy Beard had to strain, to hear anything at all.

He quickly wiped his dripping eyes, upon his tattered sleeves,
Then quietly he whispered, "I want to sail the seas,
I want to find the hidden treasures, in mystic far off lands.
I want to see amazing sights, on distant foreign sands."

I'd like a crew of furry friends, all pirates just like me,
But first I need a proper ship to sail upon the sea.
There was a tiny pat on the side of Skritchy's thigh.
The little voice spoke quietly, with a heartfelt sigh.

"I want to be first mate of a ship that sails the deep,
But I'm so small, that when I call, I hardly make a peep!"
Skritchy Beard turned around, and was very shocked to see,
A little mouse wearing sailors clothes, as small, as small could be.

"I know I'm much too small, my dream is not a mouse's sort...
But even if it's by myself, I'll sail from this old port!"
"Little mouse, you've inspired me! For that, you have my thanks!
Even though I have no crew, be first to join my ranks!"

So Mr. Squeak and Skritchy Beard went looking through some junk,
They found a wooden barrel, but the inside really stunk.
They rolled it to the ocean, and cleaned it a long time,
Scrubbing it with soap and sand, to get out all the grime.
At last, the barrel sparkled, as only scrubbed wood can,
Full of gleaming promise, and they moved on with their plan.

"She's a beauty Captain. I feel adventure in the air.
Let's get her in the ocean, and see just how she'll fare."
It took the two an hour, to get her in the water right,
But in the end, she floated well, and was a pretty sight.
Eagerly, they climbed aboard, a pirate mouse and cat,
Ready for a life at sea, full of treasure and all that!

Their barrel caught a current, and it floated day and night.
It wasn't very long at all 'til the land was out of sight.
That's when the two friends realized, with a little bit of fear,
While the ocean was quite pretty... They had no food out here!
The water was too salty for either one to drink.
Quite concerned, the two sat down, to have a good long think.

"This is bad!" said Skritchy Beard, sounding all depressed.
"Look!" Mr. Squeak shouted, seeming quite distressed.
The water all around them began to dance and leap.
Full of churning, burbling bubbles, foaming from the deep.
Their little pirate barrel boat suddenly seemed to rise,
As the largest turtle ever rose up before their eyes!

His shell was like a mountain, if mountains moved about,
His size could rival islands, when measured tail to snout.
Among the crags and ridges, of that ponderous, massive shell,
Lay countless shipwrecked vessels, that to oceans' bottom fell.
They had a perfect view, from that barnacled mountain peak,
And saw a sight that cheered them up,
and made things look less bleak.

A little island village, lay not that far away,
If they had a wooden paddle, they could be there in a day.
Skritchy Beard and Mr. Squeak ran searching through the wrecks,
Looking for a paddle, on those broken wooden decks.
The little mouse found a paddle, and slowly brought it back,
Skritchy Beard found coins, in a moldy, burlap sack.

The pirates paddled for a day before they reached the shore,
And ran straight into a restaurant, crashing through the door.
The waiter inside rushed on over, his customers to greet,
But when he saw a cat and mouse, he tossed them on the street.
Skritchy Beard and Mr. Squeak both feared this was the end,
When they heard a quiet whisper, from behind a garbage bin.

"Hey there mates, you seem quite hungry, so if both you don't mind,
The name's Big Wally, I'm a cook, would you like some food of mine?"
"We'd love a meal," said Skritchy Beard. Mr. Squeak said, "CHEESE!"
Skritchy Beard just shook his head, "He meant to say, 'Yes please.'"
"Right, no problem, let's see what's on the menu today,"
And Wally jumped right in the trash, and began to dig away.

He pulled up lots of different things, he even found some cheese,
And despite his very hefty girth, he moved about with ease.
His technique looked like dancing, all around his tiny pot,
As he dumped in everything, from the trash that he had got.
The pinch of spice he added to that wretched, stinking stew,
Worked some kind of magic, as it changed to something new!

Its color changed from greasy black to a hue of gleaming gold,
Its burning rubber smell, became something savory-bold.
Skritchy Beard and Mr. Squeak stared in utter shock,
And as he passed out steaming bowls, their host began to talk.
"You two have warmed me fuzzy heart, and I'm glad we three could meet.
Sadly though I am a chef, whose food no one will eat."

Skritchy Beard and Mr. Squeak, ate 'til it was all gone,
And as the two had their fill, Big Wally carried on.
"Ever since I was a kitten, I've always loved to cook,
But no matter how it tasted, no one could stand the look.
They said it was disgusting, and they simply kicked me-owt.
No one would try me cooking, until you came about."

Skritchy Beard and Mr. Squeak, both looked at one another,
"My name's Captain Skritchy Beard, this mouse is like my brother.
He is first mate Mr. Squeak, and we have a deal for you,
If you'd like to be our cook, you can join our pirate crew!"
Wally looked so happy, as his eyes lit up with pleasure,
"Cooking aboard a pirate ship, would please me beyond measure!"

Wally whistled happily, as he packed up his supplies,
"Let's go back to your ship and meet the other guys!"
Mr. Squeak looked at the ground, and Skritchy coughed contritely,
"I'm afraid it's just us three," he responded quite politely.
Wally looked a bit confused, and asked for more detail,
"Your ship's not very big if it only took you two to sail."

So they walked down to the beach, to see their pirate boat,
Wally stared, and asked in shock, "Does it even float?"
"I know it's not that great a ship," said Skritchy with a sigh.
Mr. Squeak said defensively, "We gave it our best try!"
"If we're going to sail the sea, this barrel just won't do,
And with a bigger vessel, we need a proper crew!"

"Very well," said Skritchy Beard, "I have some coins to spend."
"We need wood, rope, and a sail, along with some more friends."
Mr. Squeak to Wally asked, "Do you know of anyone?"
"I'm afraid when people see me, they all tend just to run."
"Okay," said Captain Skritchy Beard, "the crew will have to wait."
"For now we need a better ship, this one's a sorry state."

"Mr. Squeak, find us some rope, Wally can find a sail."
"I'll go find some wood, a hammer, and a bag of nails."
Mr. Squeak went to the docks, while Wally searched the trash,
Skritchy Beard went to the town, with their little bit of cash.
The docks were all deserted, except for a single kitty fishin',
Mr. Squeak ran boldly up, a mouse upon a mission.

"Excuse me, sir, I see you're busy, but some rope is all I need,
I'm on a quest for Captain Skritchy, and I must succeed!"
The fishing cat looked grumpy, as he tugged upon his line,
"Sorry mouse, I have some rope, but I'm afraid it's mine.
And anyway, you little mouse, my rope's too much for you,
But out of curiosity, what were you going to do?"

"We're going to build a pirate ship, in which to sail the seas,
And live our lives as pirates, doing everything we please."
The fishing cat reeled in his line, then slowly turned around,
"My name is Kitty Stokes, and my fishing skills astound.
I've fished these waters since my birth, caught every type of fish,
To cast in far off oceans, would be my one true wish."

"Come on mouse, let's get my rope, I want to meet your crew,
And ask this Captain Skritchy, if I can sail with you."
Meanwhile, in the part of town, where wood is cut to size,
Skritchy Beard, the pirate cat, was searching for his prize.
He needed lots of lumber, some hammers, and some nails,
Without a lot to spend, he was looking for some sales.

It took him several hours, but he got it all at last,
Lots of lumber, bags of nails, some hammers, and a mast.
And as he started dragging this prize back to his friends,
A wheezy voice called out to him, from just around the bend.
"If you're heading to the beach, you're going the wrong way."
Skritchy turned to give his thanks, but was lost for what to say.

The lonely cat that spoke to him, was sitting closely by,
Wearing two black eye-patches, one covering each eye.
"I know what you must think, my friend, to see my sorry face,
You're wondering all about me, and what I'm doing in this place.
I'll tell you my sad story, if you care to hang about,
I used to be a navigator, 'til they threw me-owt!"

"I had two strikes against me, for one I was a cat,
I was also blind since birth, who can navigate like that?
Well, let me tell you something, as I've often said,
I can tell direction, with the compass in me head!
I can point to north or south, or east or west now too.
Oh, by the way, the name's Blind Tom, now tell me about you."

Skritchy Beard was quite impressed, and shouted out with glee,
"I'm a pirate captain, you can navigate for me!
We're building up a pirate ship, and gathering a crew!
And if you feel like sailing, we've got a spot for you!"
"Your offer sounds amazing, I accept with all me heart.
I can't wait to point the way for you, to distant foreign parts."

So Skritchy Beard and Blind Tom brought the wood all back,
While Wally fetched some dirty sails he found under some sacks.
Mr. Squeak and Kitty Stokes brought them lots of rope,
They stared at all their ship supplies, full of rising hope.
Hellos and dreams were shared, there upon the beach.
Each could feel his deepest wish was suddenly in reach.

And so they started working, with all their new supplies,
Their ship of dreams was taking shape right before their eyes.
The mast was kind of crooked, and the hull was sort of weird,
But that ship looked simply purr-fect to Captain Skritchy Beard!
And as the sun was setting, and the stars came twinkling out,
Those fuzzy little pirates gave a happy, hearty shout!

Skritchy Beard started speaking, to his crew upon the beach,
"Everybody told us, our dreams were out of reach!"
They told us kitties couldn't sail, nor mice be a first mate!
They told us kitties couldn't cook, nor blindly navigate!
Well, we have shown them all already, with this ship we did create,
That anyone can reach their dreams, it's not all up to fate!"
With those words the crew set sail, for treasure, fun, and glory,
But, dear readers, those adventures are for another story.

Claim Your FREE Gift!
Visit
PDICBooks.com/Gift

Thank you for purchasing
Skritchy Beard
and welcome to the Puppy Dogs & Ice Cream
family.
We're certain you're going to love the little gift
we've prepared for you at the website above.

CPSIA information can be obtained
at www.ICGtesting.com
Printed in the USA
BVHW020105010522
635786BV00019B/193

9 781955 151634